Brutal Honesty

Brutal Honesty
by Leonard Chivers

ISBN: 978-0-6151-4051-3

For additional information regarding Brutal Honesty, please email honestybrutal@yahoo.com.

To purchase the electronic version of Brutal Honesty, or to order additional paperback copies, please visit www.lulu.com/brutalhonesty.

Published by Leonard Chivers 2007

Contents

Prologue

To me, life is about truth and being free, to have the free will to think and speak out about how you feel. It's always good to speak your mind as long as there is truth to what you're saying and if you feel it's the right thing to say at the right time. When you do say what's on your mind, there has to be respect to the people you talk to. A lot people tell me I'm rude or insensitive, but that's not how I see myself. I see myself as speaking the truth and being honest about what I say. I will never bullshit you, no matter what it's about. And if I'm wrong, I would be the first to say I'm sorry.

When I was growing up I saw a lot of shit that made me sick. Today there is so much more shit added to the world by people that it just doesn't make any sense. I don't understand how people can be so blind to it or simply not care. Some people are afraid to say what's on their minds. Why? Because they might offend someone or hurt their feelings. Who cares? I look at it as if you care for someone enough, you should have the heart to let him or her know how you feel and what you're thinking, but to always show respect to that person.

For example, if I don't like some of the religious beliefs that people tell me about, I'm going to let those people know how I feel. If I have to stand there and listen to what they're saying, when they're done it's my turn. Sometimes people can't handle it. I'm not doing it to be an ass or to belittle anyone. It's just me sharing my beliefs, and if they don't like it I don't care. If I had to listen to them, it will be their turn to hear me out.

I guess that in life I can't sit back and watch the stupid shit and the ignorant way people deal with it. It's like some people have no life other then to sit there and complain about what other people do in their own lives and how they live it. So now, I feel it's my job to let everyone know how I feel about some of their beliefs and opinions. Let's see how they handle what someone has to say about them.

There is so much in life that people don't want to open their eyes to and see, and now I'm here to tell the world what I think. There will be truth to what I say and it will be brutal, and it will hit you hard. You may feel that I have no heart, but oh well. It's all truth from my point of view.

We all know that there are sensitive people in the world. You may feel like I'm bringing you or your family down. That's not what I'm trying to do. I want the people of today to see the way things look from another perspective, and what can be done to fix this world, or just to fix what we have in our own homes.

Life can be harder on some people then it is on others. I just want to share my views on life and how we live it. For years I've had family and friends tell me that I should have been a lawyer because I argue a point to the end. They've told me I should have my own radio show, thinking the listeners would get a kick out of me. Finally, people say I should just have my own talk show on TV. I just want to write this book to let all the readers know my opinions and the truth behind them. There are over sixty issues in life that I have strong opinions on. They may make you laugh, upset you or down right piss you off. If I hit a nerve or two then I did my job. It will show that I'm right and that we need to take care of some things in life.

Some people won't be able to handle what they are about to read. Others will say this guy has a point. So please kick back and enjoy the opinions of one man.

<u>Warning</u>

To the people who don't have an open mind or common sense, or if you are over sensitive, please do not continue past this point.

Pedophiles and Molesters

I shouldn't have to say much about these people, but unfortunately in the world today it's getting bad for all of our kids. I'm tired of seeing these people get a few years in jail and then released, put back into our society. They go out and do it again, but now you hear about them brutally raping or even killing a child. Then they get life in prison.

You know what? Forget that. If someone is that sick that they have to molest or rape a child then they should automatically get the death penalty. That's right, put them to death. They don't need to go to jail and get help for what they have done. There is no help for people like that. They're sick and twisted individuals. Still, give them their day in court. When they are found 100% guilty, that's it, death for them. Take them out back and shoot them for all I care. Don't put them on death row. There is nothing to appeal. You did it, you hurt or killed a child. You should be put to death, no waiting. And I don't mean put the 17 and 18 year olds to death for having sex with a 15 or 16 year old. That's just teenage love and there is nothing we can do about that. Remember, we were all teenagers once and we really do know what it's like.

But people say that these pedophiles should go to jail and think about what they've done. That's a bunch of crap. What about the little kids and families that are scarred for life? The criminal gets out in a few years and lives their life the way they want. Oh yeah, they have to register with the state. Who cares? They still run free while the families are devastated for life. I hope that one day our children can play outside and we won't have to worry as much that someone is going to kidnap them, take them somewhere and rape them, leaving them to die.

I know someone whose daughter was molested. She called the state for help and they gave the woman a lawyer and they gave her children a lawyer, because in our state that's how it's done. That was great. She won custody of the kids and the guy went to jail for a long time, though he should have gotten the death penalty. But anyway, after all was said and done, she got a bill from the state saying that she has to pay for the lawyers used in the case. With hardly any money coming in, they told her it was court ordered for her to pay.

Let me get this right. Some sick pervert molested his daughter and got his jollies off, and now the mother has to pay for the lawyer that the state said she and the kids had to have? That's just wrong. I think that sick pervert should have to pay, not the victims. The victim and their families have to go through enough without the courts saying they can go to jail if they don't pay.

This country needs wake up and smell what it's shoveling.

Racism

Here is something that there will be no end to unless people really take a good look at how they treat each other. In today's world we need to be more open minded and less worried about skin color.

When people look at each other they see color, they see another race. Come on, get over it. Black, White, Asian or Arabic, we are all human beings, that's it. We pump blood through our hearts, we bleed when we're cut, we are all the same. When we can all look past color this will be a better world.

To the Arabics who think they are mistreated when they get pulled over by the police... When they find a ton of cell phones, a lot of money and pictures of land marks, you'll be looked at as someone who is up to no good. Don't blame the men and women who are doing their job to keep America safe. Blame your own people that like to blow shit up for a cause.

I'm sorry, but it's true. You don't see blacks or whites or hispanics blowing shit up for a cause. They organize and march through the streets with pride, and to me that's awesome. They're proving a point without people getting killed.

In my eyes I see all men as equals. If someone does something to you that you don't like, blame the man that did it, not the race of the man. That's a good start of getting rid of racism.

Gas Prices

What gets me about gas prices is that I see the prices at the pump go up for days and then back down, and then up again. Why is this? Because the price of a barrel went up. Who cares? The gas is still under the ground at the gas stations, and they raised the price at the pump for the price of a barrel that won't reach the gas stations for 6 months. This is a bunch of crap. Why should the pump prices go up before the barrels reach us?

I guess it's a good way for them to make a lot of money from us, the stupid people that don't ask questions. Why don't we strike against the gas companies? If everyone in America would use their heads and not buy gas for one week, they'd be forced to lower their prices. If everyone did that the gas companies will lose millions of dollars.

Why don't the big wigs at the gas companies use *their* heads for once and help the people, instead of trying to rape us for our pay checks? If the prices change for a barrel of oil, they should wait to jack up the prices until *after* all the gas is gone at the pumps. When they refill the tanks at the gas stations, then they should raise the prices. I'm tired of watching the prices change twice a day.

But we all know who makes the big money off the gas prices, and if you don't know, guess what? I'm going to give you a clue. Oh, what the hell, I'll tell you. It's our good old President George W. Bush. He is in his last term of his presidency and I think someone wants to make a lot of money before they're gone. But I could be wrong, that's just my thoughts on it.

Religious Beliefs

Why do people slam other people's religious beliefs? Well guess what, I'm going to tell you. Because they have nothing better to do. If people don't like it when a manger is displayed during Christmas time, get over it and don't look at it. If you do not like taking medicines when you're sick then that's your choice. Suffer then. But when I'm sick and I know that taking something will help me, guess what, I'm taking it. And it is not going to kill my soul.

Why do some religions think I'm going to hell? Let me guess, because you think I'm not saved. How do you know what I am? What gives you the right to judge me? People need to mind their own business. I think when it all comes down to it there is only one God and he has forgiven all of us.

Oh my god, the money in the United States has "in God we trust" and some of you people are freaking out! Get over it jackass. We don't have to change our money for you. If you don't like it, tough shit. And let's not forget about the people who want us to stop talking about God in our schools. It's been like that for years, and if you don't like it then try home schooling your kids. What I'm trying to say is that if you have your beliefs, that's great. Keep it in your church and in your homes and don't worry about what other people are doing.

To the Islamic, sorry for what the pope said, but look at what you're doing. My god, that isn't a way to protest, rioting and burning churches. You just helped him prove his point. I mean, if everyone who reads this book says stuff about me, does that mean I can go out and riot, burn schools and people's homes? Come on people, get over it! It's only words by one man. Grow up and be better then that.

Just remember that people came here to get away from religious persecution, so I say live and let live. You have your beliefs and we have ours. No one tells you how to enjoy that freedom, and we don't need anyone telling us what to believe and how to decorate in our religious celebrations.

People Who Eat

I don't want to be mean about it, but come on, quit eating so much! I know some people have a medical problem and they can't help gaining weight. Then there are people out there that just need to cut down on how much they eat.

Guess what, all soda pop is going to add pounds to you. Just because it says diet doesn't mean you're going to lose weight. My god, look at what you're eating! It's not all good for you. Watch what you eat and don't eat so much of it. I see people eat 2 or 3 helpings of food plus dessert, and then wash it down with a diet coke. It doesn't work that way. Everyone who eats like that will eventually gain weight and have heart problems. Their knees will hurt and their backs will ache because of their stomachs. They'll even develop high blood pressure and suffer more serious health problems because of over eating.

Come on, America. It's time to stop shoving all that fast food down our throats and start eating healthier. I mean, watch what you eat and eat smaller portions. We aren't getting any younger. The older we get the harder it is to shed the pounds. Believe me, I can't fit into half my clothes after this year of double cheeseburgers and pizza.

People Who Smell

Ok, please don't take this to heart. I really do know some people have active glands and they can't help that they smell. But to the ones that just don't shower or take baths, please start taking showers and use the soap. My god, we don't want to smell you anymore!

You know who you are. If we can smell you then I know you can smell yourself. When you start to smell like your own urine, please go wash yourself. It sucks when I'm at the grocery store and smell nothing but urine or really bad body odor. I just want to leave, and guess why. Because I just lost my appetite.

So please, if you smell yourself, go take a shower. Use soap and deodorant. It will help you! People won't mind you standing by them when you talk to them, and you just might make a few new friends.

People with bad breath, please just go brush your teeth and use mouthwash. Then the people you date just might want to give you that goodnight kiss. If you drink coffee or smoke like I do, then you know what I'm talking about. I brush my teeth twice a day just so I have a fresh mouth, because I never know who I might run into and want to give that person a big kiss hello.

People's Driving

This first part goes out to the stupid people that can't handle talking on a cell phone and driving a straight line. Hang up the damn phone if you can't pay attention to the roads. How hard is it for you to understand that driving and cell phones don't mix? You know, when you're at a red light you can dial the phone then, instead of swerving into other people's lanes. My god, just use your heads. I'm really going to give you people crap now. When you're driving and the speed limit sign shows its 50, do the damn speed limit. If you can't drive and be on your cell phone, hang the damn thing up and drive. I get stuck behind people who are doing 35 in a 50 and that really pisses me off. Stay home to talk instead of doing it on the roads.

Why is it that if you honk your horn at someone to speed up, they look in their rearview mirror and give you the finger? Then the road rage starts. Gee, I wonder why there are so many accidents out there. People just don't care about other drivers. If people take the time to look around when they make a lane change instead of talking on their phone, the accident rate just might drop.

There was this one jerk that cut my wife off, so she honked the horn at the guy. He stuck his finger up at my wife so my wife gave him the finger back. Then the guy had the nerve to want to fight my wife, telling her to pull over and fight. My god, what kind of a jackass wants to start a fight with a woman? Especially when she was cut off by *him* and just honked her horn! I hope he feels like a real man now, wanting to beat up a woman. My god people, if everyone would use their heads when they drive, we all would be better off.

To all the drunk drivers, stay off the damn roads when you drink. Who gives you the right to take other peoples lives? I think if you drink and drive and kill someone you should get the death penalty.

And to the senior citizens, if you can't do the speed limit, if you can't make that turn, if you start parking on sidewalks or smashing through buildings and running over a bunch of people in a parking lot, I think it's time for you to hand in your driver's license and start taking the smart bus. I'm only telling you the truth. I see too many accidents, and I don't want you to hurt yourselves or anybody else.

Our Government

I could be here a lifetime talking about this, but I'll just sum it up as much as I can. Let's start with our great President of the United States of America, George W. Bush. He did do one thing right, fighting terrorists. I think he was a little slow from the get go, but he did start fighting back.

I'm sorry, but if I were the President I would have sent bombs to destroy the countries that harbored terrorist the next day, and don't tell me they need to find out who was behind it. Let's see, the country that was singing and dancing in the streets while burning an American flag would be the first clue.

Why wait? They didn't care who was in our buildings and planes. I think we should have just made a parking lot out of those countries and renamed it the Middle East of the United States. And there you go, no more terrorists. Sure we would have people saying stuff about us, but they'll get it over it. Why do people think our country is so bad because we have freedom? My god, what makes us so different? If we have millions of illegal immigrants dying or trying to come into our country it can't be all that bad.

I do think that our country should take care of our own people, like the elderly, the sick, and the mentally ill. Giving our money to help other countries, why? We need help here, this is just stupid. They say that the crime rates go up every year. Let's see why. Because our government lets the jobs go over seas and people are losing their jobs here left and right. Help keep our jobs in America so people can feed their families, keep the heat and electricity on and keep a roof over their heads.

And what about our kids? They need special surgeries to help them walk better, look better, or to keep them alive and all I hear is that you have to have insurance to get the surgeries done. Come on government, help our kids. I see people fly into the United States so they can have special surgeries for themselves or one of their kids and we the taxpayers pay for it. What about helping our kids in need when families can't afford it? Who gives you the right to send our money we pay in taxes ever year to other countries when we need the help here?

Smoking in Public

Why do people have to whine so much about smoking? Why are they prohibiting smoking in restaurants and other business? My god people, just shut the hell up. I think the business owners should be the ones to determine if people can smoke. Who gives the government the right to step in? If people don't want to be by smokers, just stay home.

I was in a restaurant the other day and after I ate my meal I lit up a smoke. The next thing I hear is some crybaby whining that they smell smoke and it's bothering them. Well you know what? Too damn bad. If you don't like the smell, get out. Cook your meal at home or go to a non-smoking restaurant.

I think the restaurants make more money from smokers then non-smokers anyway. And what about the bars? We all know that if they make people stop smoking there they will lose so much money. My god, just leave things alone.

The government should let all of the business owners decide who can smoke and who can't. The government makes more money on taxes from all of us smokers then the non-smokers, and now they want to start banning smoking all over the place. We pay enough money in taxes, so I think we can smoke wherever the hell we want. The government needs to stay on one side of the line, not both sides. They tell us where we can smoke and then raise the prices by adding higher taxes because they want to make more money off of us. You know what? Let the people vote on it, and then we will see what happens.

Healthcare

First off, the government should help all families with the cost of health insurance. Why you ask? Well let me tell you. When the government can pay millions of dollars to make a missile that can find the heart beat of a person and blow them up, I think they can spend some of that money on the people that can't pay for health insurance.

Or you know, there is another way we can come up with a plan to get everyone in America health insurance. The government could talk to all the corporations that make billions of dollars off of us each year, and give them a tax break when each corporation donates two million dollars a year in a fund for the people of America. That's right a fund to help each family in America get health insurance. Make it a fund that the government itself can't touch like they do the social security funds. We all know the corporations can help do this. If they say it would hurt them to donate, I think they would be full of shit. After they make billions of dollars in profits, they can help this country that helped make them become rich. That just might be a good start for this country's turn around for the people.

Look at what else is happening in today's world of health care with companies that want to get out of paying for their employees. I know a woman who works for a big company that makes millions of dollars a year, I mean millions. And now they just cut their health care benefits. They have to pay out of pocket for the total price of prescriptions and office visits, but they said they will put money in an account for the works, about $1200.00 a year. Who cares? People spend more then that on prescriptions in a year, not to mention the office visits that can range from $35.00 to $80.00 a visit. And for the average family, that's a lot of money.

You know some of these insurance companies make me sick. If I want to quit smoking the insurance company doesn't want to help pay the $120.00 for the pills or the patches or gum so I can quit. But, if I get that tumor in me, they'll help pay the bigger dollars to save me. Why not just help the people who want to quit smoking and they'll save money in the long run. But I guess it's easier to pay $25,000.00 to help get rid of a tumor then it is to pay $120.00 to help us quit smoking. No wonder why the cost of health insurance is so high.

And if the hospitals stop charging $35.00 for an aspirin or $20.00 for a band-aid, maybe the cost of health insurance could go down a little more. But that's just me thinking out loud.

Cell Phones

Why do all the cell phone providers charge so much money for a stupid cell phone? They charge us a monthly rate, which is kind of fair. But if you want text messages they charge an arm and a leg. Come on, give us a break. They get to charge us state use tax, then a state sales tax, plus an operational 911 fee. And don't forget the fed universal fee, regulatory fee and the administrative charge. Which by the way, we have to pay every month for.

Ok, what the hell is a state use tax? That should be covered under our plan we paid for. But I guess it's a way to make money every time we hit that send button. Now for the state sales tax we pay for every month. That should have been a one time charge when we bought our cell phones and plans, and not have to pay a sales tax every month. We paid for that when we bought the service plan, and we should just have to pay for service until our contract is up. The operational 911 fee they charge should have been in the price of the total plan we got and not have to pay every month.

This is just stupid that we have to pay for a total of 6 different taxes every month. Don't they make enough money off their packages that we pay for? Don't get me wrong, I love my cell phone and can't live without it. But give us, the little people, a break.

The Internet

The internet is the most wonderful and excellent tool to help us learn, pay our bills on line, do our banking and even to find that special someone who is out there for us. And it also can ruin your life in a second. If someone gets your passwords, you're done. Your money can be stolen from you in a blink of an eye. People can steal your identity and the bills can pile up for you. Even your family's lives can be smashed in seconds if your spouse finds himself or herself an internet lover, running off to be with the man or woman of their dreams. And then they realize, "Wow, I screwed up! I'll just go back home and fix it with my spouse."

Yeah, right. I know one guy that has a great job and is making a lot of money while the wife stays home and takes care of the house and kids. I think that is a great thing for them. The husband does have to travel once in a while and he is gone for two to three days at a time. So one day the wife goes online and finds herself an internet lover. The guy talks the wife into leaving her husband and kids to go move in with him. That almost destroyed the husband and it really did hurt the kids. Do you want to know what the wife's excuse was? She had the nerve to say her husband doesn't spend enough time with her and it's his fault she had to leave. Let me get this right... The husband had to travel for work and busted his ass off to make excellent money so they could live in a huge house with awesome cars, and so that she could shop all the time, spending his money. He didn't care what she bought as long as the bills were paid. And now he's the asshole for going to work? It's his fault for bringing the money home so they can have the life for their kids that they never had? Wow, that guy is a jerk. Whoever would think of a guy neglecting his wife by going to work so she can have a life of her dreams? I hope that the internet lover gave her what she was missing. Oh wait, he did. He was a bum that lived with his mom, collecting an S.S. check every month and he has all the time in the world to spend with her. God bless the internet.........

Divorce

Well here is a great topic, right? Everyone that I know that divorced told me the major reason for it was other people putting their noses where they don't belong. My god people, stay out of other peoples business. You know as soon as the in-laws and friends put their fat noses in other people's marriages, it's over. Why can't people just stay out and let the other people handle what's going on in their own marriages? But no one can do that. They think they're helping but they're not.

Let me tell you about a guy I know. He was having problems with his wife. Not serious problems, but they were financial. They were going to try to work it out, but all the shit hit the fan when her parents got involved. They took her to lawyer, not even giving the guy a chance to tell his side of the story. What gets me the most is that the next-door neighbor even put her nose into their business, and she didn't even know what was going on.

What happened was one day after work this guy decided to drive by his wife's house to see the kids. He was happy to see them. He saw that the wife had made a roast beef dinner and he asked to have some. The wife told him, "No, you can't have any." She was mad at him. Ok, I can understand that. So the guy left and went to his apartment that was only 2 miles down the road. He went inside, took a shower, and wondered what to get for dinner. Next thing he knew, his phone rang. It was one of his friends, and yes, it was a woman. She said she had gotten a loan and paid off all her bills. She had some money left over and she was taking her kids out to dinner to celebrate. Her kids asked if he could go with them, so the guy said yes.

Anyway, the guy jumped in his car and met them at Red Lobster. They sat at a big round table, with the guy at one side and the lady friend at the other side, and each child at her sides. After dinner the guy said thank you and went home. The next day he got a phone call. It was his wife yelling and screaming at him. She said the neighbor's brother was at Red Lobster eating dinner and he said he saw the guy kissing all over the woman and hanging on her. Well, that was it. The in-laws took her to a lawyer and had the papers drawn up, not even giving the guy a chance to defend himself.

After all was said and done they got the divorce. The man said he didn't want anything from the house, because he didn't want take anything away from his children. The man walked away from a 10 year marriage with a $600.00 a month child support payment.

Months after the divorce the neighbor that had her nose in the middle of everything told the truth and said her brother just saw the guy eating dinner with the woman and then he left. So like I say, people need to keep their big noses out of other people's business, because that neighbor just helped ruin a 10 year marriage by being a fat pain in the ass. And why do I know so much about this guy? Because it was me.

Child Support

I'm glad that in the world today they crack down on the dead beat parents that don't help take care of their children. I support that 100%. Every women or man deserves that check every week. But here is what I have a problem with. Friend of the Court looks at every *dad* as a dead beat. Why is that? I myself pay child support, and when I go down there they treat me like shit. I'm not the only guy they do that to either. Our rights are for shit. I was told years ago when I started paying child support that they would send a court order to my boss and have the money taken out of my check every week, which I thought was cool. But after a month they hadn't taken any money out, so I decided to go down to Friend of the Court and find out what was going on. And oh man, was I treated like dirt. The case worker had an attitude from the moment he called my name. When I walked up to him at the counter he started yelling at me "Why haven't you started paying? Where are your checks? Do you want to go to jail?" I was in a daze. I felt belittled. I told the guy "I was told they were going to send a court order to my boss to deduct it out of my check." Then he started yelling at me for nearly three minutes about how I should have just sent in a check myself. He was chastising me for it. After this guy's face got all red from yelling at me like a jackass, I told him "I did pay the woman in cash until you morons said you'd deduct the money from my check." Then he yelled, "Where is the proof that you paid the mother?" So I pulled out 6 receipts and showed him, to which he replied "Oh, good."

So then I looked at him and said, "That's all you have to say to me is 'good'? After all the shit you gave me about going to jail, and that I don't pay? What kind of are place are you running here?" I told him, "I came here of my own freewill to find out why they aren't deducting money from my check, and I get treated like an asshole." Figure that one out. The Friend of the Court is a bunch of high paid nobody's that need to get their heads out of their asses and treat the guys that do pay and pick up their kids every weekend with a little more respect.

Music of Today

Everyone said Elvis is the king of rock "n" roll. Ok, he's dead now, and after a king dies they crown a new one. So I think its time to crown a new one for rock "n" roll. Really, who would be king of today's music?

There are so many to choose from. Marilyn Manson, Kid rock, Van Halen, AC-DC, or even Eminem. Ok, I know he's hip-hop, but you get my point. The music world has to pick a new king of rock "n" roll, but it would be hard to.

Today's music is awesome. We have a much better variety of music, from rock, hip-hop, R&B and much more. But why do people come down on the music of today? Because they sing about truth. They let the world know what they think about or how they live life.

I think it's cool when a music artist, rapper or anyone who has nothing, goes through life catching their dreams. They're fighting through shit just to get there, then they make their CD and all of a sudden people start freaking out about what they're saying.

Come on, its only music and they're singing about their life, and people want to ban them.

I can't wait to see when generation X starts running this country. I hope they take the age ban off all of the music labels. Why? Because if you hold things back from your kids, they're just going to download it or find a way to listen to it anyway. Why ban it? Because you think swearing is bad? Yet they hear it everyday at school or even in the home with their parents.

If you don't like it, just don't listen to it. To all the churches that try to ban music, go read your Bible and say your prayers and ask God to forgive you for judging others.

Our Cable Television

Here's something that someone is making billions of dollars a year on. I know cable television is great TV, but come on, why do we have to pay to watch TV? Just to get local channels with a good reception we have to pay.

Ok, I know we should have to pay for the movie channels and I'm ok with that. But to watch all of the regular stations, we have to pay for that also. That's wrong. Don't you think that all the networks that are out there should be the ones to pay the cable company to broadcast them, and not charge us to watch them? They will make tons more money doing it that way.

To the networks, which have all the advertisers that they want, advertisement is a big money maker for them. To be broadcast all over the world is even bigger money. So why don't those networks pay the cable company? We all know the name of our cable provider, who has monopolized the country. Since we have no other choices, let those networks help pay. Why should we all go broke? To watch TV?

That goes for the satellite companies as well. I will admit one thing though. Cable is a lot better then a satellite dish. When the weather gets cloudy or two inches of snow, you lose signal. What a joke.

School Dress Codes

Wow, what can I say about school dress codes? For one thing guys, pull your damn pants up. No one wants to see your underwear. You may think you look cool but you don't. You look like a bunch of jackasses that I wouldn't trust with a potato gun. Come on, have pride in the way you look.

And for the girls, we think you don't need to show off your thongs. You don't need to show off your stomach to show how cool you are, and no one wants to see your ass crack. Just go to class and get an education.

I will say some schools need to relax on the clothes issue though. If a shirt has a figure on it or a saying that really isn't that bad, you need to leave it alone. If a student is wearing a tank top and nothing is popping out of it, leave that alone as well. You school districts cause more problems then anything. Let the kids make their statement with what they wear. Just because you don't like it doesn't mean it's not a legitimate style. I see kids in our school district wearing Goth pants with chains on them, and the schools around here don't like it.

Oh well, get over that to. The chains are mostly sewn on anyways. It's just a fashion statement.

What Parents Need to Know

I'm no expert on this subject, but then again, who is? I will tell you, if you keep an open honest relationship with your kids and learn to trust each other, you and your kids would be set for life.

I find it easy to communicate with all six of my children, ages 2, 7, 9, 13, 15, and 16. I know, what can I say? I love kids. One thing I do know is that if you're open to them, they will talk to you about everything. The trick is to totally be honest with them.

One day my 16 year old came up to me and asked me about drugs. I was shocked. One day they're into video games and the next thing they're asking about drugs. I thought it was cool that he knew to come to me first. I didn't freak out on him, I just asked "What would you like to know?" He asked what marijuana does to you if you smoke it. I sat back and told him it would really fry your brain cells and make you very sleepy, and after a while you will get the munchies.

Then I said, "May I ask you a question?" He said sure. I asked if he had tried it. He told me no, and then said some friends had offered it to him. I just told him that when he's out there where we can't always keep an eye on him, he will have to make some of the biggest decisions of his life. I told him that he really better think of the consequences if he does drugs. If he gets caught he's going to jail, and I told him I wouldn't bail him out. If he gets caught in school with it, he's done. His education just went out the window. I told him to take a hard look at what it can do to himself and his family, because if he decides to be a druggie he knows he's out of the house. After an hour of talking, not yelling or screaming about it, he just said "Thanks Dad." And now we talk about everything.

I have one son and five daughters. I don't want to see anything bad happen to them so I make sure we all sit down and talk about everything, even sex. I told the older girls that we are not always going to be there to guide them, so they better use their heads. They do know one thing that I always tell them… no glove, no love. I don't want them having babies at a young age. Instead of freaking out and making them hate me, we sat down and had a talk about everything from babies to sexual transmitted diseases, and how their lives can change in a blink of an eye, just for one night of fun.

I know it's not easy talking to your kids. Just remember, try to be open, honest and truthful, and the rest will take care of itself. And one more thing, when you do talk to your kids it's easy to sit there and criticize them, but remember they also need to hear the words "I'm proud of you." You will be surprised how well they do when they hear that once in a while.

Debt Collectors

Ah, one of life's biggest harassments, the great old debt collectors. You know, it's funny when these people call. They think they're playing God when they threaten us with lawsuits and the garnishing of our wages. I know they can garnish our wages for not paying our bills, but the lawsuit part gets me.

Come on, all they do is take it to your local courts and they get the judgment saying, yes, you owe to that company money, and yes, you have to pay them. Then they rack up court fees and now you have to pay that too. Do you think some of these companies would work with us?

Here is a little something you didn't know. If you offer a debt collector $15.00 or even $25.00, they have to take it. They can't turn your money away. They just try to get more from you. If they ever turn you down you can tell them you're going to report them to the Better Business Bureau for not taking your money.

What I've heard is that the Better Business Bureau will sometimes help erase the debt for you, because of the company threatening you and not taking your money. I'm not saying they'll erase everything, but I did have a friend that called the Better Business Bureau and got help because of the debt collector refusing to take his money. Some help is better then no help.

It's always better to protect yourself, but if you can help it, please pay your bills. Don't get anything on credit if you can't afford it. Why make things worse for yourself?

Tattoos and Piercing

What can I say? Tattoos are awesome. I have 13 and going for a few more. Some people say tattoos will ruin your skin, or they make you look stupid. Well, you know what? To hell with them. I think they look great and the tattoo artists I found at American Pride Tattoos in Berkley, Michigan are awesome. I just want to say thanks to Jennifer & Steve. You guys rock.

I have decent size tattoos for a great price. One thing about tattoos is that they help express the way you are and even tell a lot about a person. I did go in one day for a tattoo, just one. My brother Roy told me they were addictive and that I'd be getting more then one. Well, you know what? He was right. I love them and they look great. But before you get one, make sure the person that does it is the right artist for you, because it is permanent.

Make sure they are clean and always ask questions. I did and I found out some tattoo shops just reuse their needles. That's scary. I asked at American Pride Tattoo and they do not reuse needles. Every time they tattoo a new one is used, and that's better for all of us.

Now the piercings. I think some piercings are cool, like the ear, eyebrow, belly, nose, tongue and even some nipples (not all!). To pierce your face up all around your lips, that's just crazy. But if you're happy with it, I'm happy for you. Just don't go to any job interviews with all those piercings in your face. You just might scare the employer.

Take Pride in Your Home

You know what? I see a lot of people letting their homes go, and for what? So they can be the neighborhood slobs. That's right, I call them slobs. Come on, cut your grass. It doesn't take that long, and if you can't cut it, pay the neighbor kid five bucks. I bet he would cut it for you.

Really, some of you people need to stand outside of your home and say "Damn, I need to paint this house". Or edge your lawn and even weed whack. It only takes a little time and a little effort and your house and yard will look great.

To the people that have a junk yard on the front lawn, call a damn tow truck. Get rid of the junk, you don't need it. Don't you think your neighbors are saying stuff behind your back? Keep it clean. Do it for yourself, your kids and your city. Don't make it your fault that the property value is going down.

And don't take offense to this, but to my city of Detroit that I love so much, if you live next to a vacant lot and the grass is growing taller, while you're out cutting your grass have the common sense to cut the grass on the vacant lot. If everyone pitched in and did that, some of the problems you complain about will go away.

I only say this because I care. Don't make our neighborhoods look bad because you're lazy and want to be a slob. Let's all pitch in and help, and not just sitting around bitching about it blaming the city.

Michigan Jobs

I hope someday there will be a turn around in our state. We have lost so many jobs here it's ridiculous. The city that was known as the Motor City is now known as the 'steal scrap metal for money' city. All of our jobs are leaving the state and people now have to find a way to survive.

Even the new home construction business is sinking fast. I've painted for over 20 years and all of a sudden it's dead for all workers; painters, tile men, dry-wall people. I mean it. It's so bad even the Mexicans didn't come back. Now you know it's bad when that happens. I was sub-contracted so I don't get unemployment. I don't get anything, and I'm not the only one. There are so many people without jobs because of the slow down. Even the builders are giving land back to the banks.

Something needs to happen for us. People are getting tired of losing their jobs, and then watching gas prices climb to a record high. You know, it's funny how they do stuff here. You lose your job because of cut backs, yet they keep raising the prices on everything from gas to food to interest rates.

Some people have to sell their homes it's so bad. Let's just say thanks to our governor.

They say to go to this place called Michigan Works where they help you find a job. Yeah, right. I know so many people that went there and submitted resumes and not one person got a call for a job interview. All I'm saying is that if the next governor doesn't do something, we all would be in a world of hurt.

I know some people will say go work for a fast food place. Good point, but if your bills are higher then that pay check, I say keep looking for that better job or you will lose everything.

Teachers Strike

I know they strike for a good reason and I know I wouldn't want to take a pay cut. If the school district wants to cut costs they need to start at the top where the superintendent of the district makes a ton of money, and then so on down the line. Its funny, they get paid vacations, and then have most of the summer off.

Come on, help the teachers. They're the ones who do a lot more for a lot less. They're with hundreds of kids a day and you want to cut their pay? What I really don't understand is why they wait until school starts to get things done. My god, you have the whole summer to do it.

People count on the schools, because some people have to work. If their kids aren't in school they have to pay big bucks for someone to watch them. They may have to miss work, and that could cost them their jobs. Do you think it's fair to the parents who pay school taxes? No, it's not.

So I tell you what, if you work at it a little harder and not cut the teachers pay or health care, and if the big shots of the district take a small pay cut, you just might have that extra money to throw around in the right direction.

Please think about it, because our kids and their parents really do need the teachers in the classrooms, instead of staying home because you don't want to give a 1% increase in pay.

Movie Stars and Sports Stars

I love going to the movies just like anyone else, but the prices are so ridiculous. Why should we pay high prices for them to pay some actor 20 million dollars a movie? Don't get me wrong, some of the actors are really great at their jobs, but no one is worth 20 million for a 2 hour movie.

And what about some sports stars? How can they pay a ball player tons of money for grabbing his nuts and spitting on the field? I know there are great players out there, but are they really worth all that money? And we get stuck paying the high ticket prices.

I remember what my favorite hockey team in Detroit did. We all know what team that is. They paid a player about 35 million for 4 years. We all know who that was. Then the organization said, "By the way, we're raising ticket prices." For what? To see a guy score 20 goals all year and then watch him choke in the playoffs?

I'm not trying to knock all the players in sports, because you guys are great at your jobs. You bring excitement to the games you play. But do you really need to have all that money for playing school yard games? Because if that's the case, with all the ticket prices going up some of your true fans can't even afford to go to the games.

I can't wait to see how many players get upset with this one.

People Who Don't Let Other People Speak

Why is this one of the most annoying things ever? Why do people do that to each other? They never let other people speak. I hate it when people override someone and won't let them get a word in.

People need to say what they think and that's fine, but then let other people have a chance to get in a word. I've seen people sit there and ask questions of someone, and then they just keep going on, giving them crap. People need to just walk away when they're being treated this way. Don't sit there and let people walk all over you.

People need to have a chance to open up so they can express what they're thinking. If you don't give that chance to let someone speak, shame on you. That's why there is arguing, which sometimes escalates to fighting. For what? Someone that won't give the other person a chance to speak their mind.

I know that there are people out there that will sit there and just let it happen so it will be over with soon. If you let it happen, it will never stop. They will do it to you all the time just because they know you'll sit there and take it.

So you know what? It's time to grow up and let other people have a chance to express themselves. You all just might be a little happier and have a better chance of fixing the problem rather then fighting over it.

People Who Kill Over Words

What the hell is wrong with some people today? There is this local bar in our city where everyone goes to dance, see their friends and meet new people. One day this guy was at the bar having a few drinks waiting for his girlfriend. When his girlfriend walked through the door, some other guy grabbed her ass. That was it. The boyfriend went crazy over it, yelling at his girlfriend, blaming her for what some other guy did.

Anyway, they went out to the parking lot and the next thing you know he was hitting his girlfriend. You know he feels like a man when he does that. There were a couple of people walking by when he hit her, and they started yelling at the man calling him a tough guy and calling him a few other names because he was hitting a girl.

All of a sudden they started arguing, and the boyfriend pulled out a gun and shot the guy, hitting him once. The guy didn't fall so the boyfriend shot him two more times, hitting him in the chest, and the man died.

Now what I don't get is why did the boyfriend bring a damn gun to the bar? To be cool? My god, he killed someone over words. What are these people thinking when they go out to have a good time and someone brings a gun? Then he said he didn't want to kill him. Why shoot him 3 times, bonehead? Because he called you names.

First of all, don't bring your girlfriend to a bar if you don't want other guys trying to pick her up. What do you think guys are doing at bars? But most of all, people don't need to fight over words. There is enough trouble in the world without some jackass killing someone over words.

If you have to back up your words and if you're that tough, then use your fists. Or are you so scared to stand up to someone that you decide, "Hey, I have to use a gun, because it makes me feel more like a man"? When that happens you're not a man, you're a coward.

So, you know what? People are stupid that have to fight or kill someone over words. Enjoy your 20 years to life, moron.

People Who Need to Speak for Themselves

Why is it that some people won't let their friends, brother, sister or spouse say what they think? I know this one guy who won't let his wife or kids get a word in. When you ask the kids a question, he answers for them. We all know what's going to happen when the kids get older. They won't be able to speak for themselves.

It's pretty stupid that this guy is messing with his kids this way. Now that the son and daughter are older, the son thinks he has a right to talk for his sister. When I ask her a question, the brother answers for her. I told him to shut up and let his sister talk because she needs to answer for herself. The brother just looked at me like I was crazy, but I told him that if his sister doesn't learn how to speak for herself, she won't know which way to go in life or even how to make the right choices in life. You never know. She might find a guy just like her father that does all the talking for her.

Now the wife finally answers for herself and the husband doesn't like it. Well jackass, it's the 2000's. Get over it. Your family is people, not pets. If you want to be bossy get a dog. Don't use your wife and kids as pets.

Are some guys scared to let their family talk? Are you afraid they might say something about you? I think that when a person acts that way, he or she is lazy, or they don't want others knowing what they really are. Treat your family with love, not stupidity.

Double Standard

That's right women. There is a thing called a double standard and we all know you ladies hate it. I don't blame you. It's not fair that boys get to stay out later then girls and that boys get to do more things then girls.

But it's ok in my mind. I have 3 teenagers, 2 girls and 1 boy, and I do let my son stay out later then the girls. You know what? I know my son is a little safer then my girls. If someone jumps him he has a fighting chance, or he can run fast. I hate to say it, but girls can't really fight some guy off if he wants to take something from them.

My daughters do argue with me, and they won't win. I'm sorry, but I feel safer knowing my girls are in the house when it starts getting dark outside. The way things are today, there are sick perverts out there grabbing girls off the streets, even right in front of their own homes. That takes a lot of balls for someone to pull off. I just feel better knowing they're in for the night.

I don't do it to be mean, but sometimes my girls are walking by themselves and that's the scary part. If they're with a few of their friends, then I just might let them stay out a little longer, but when they're by themselves their asses are in the house when the sun goes down.

Even if they're with their boyfriend, I want them in at dark because I know what teenage girls are like today. I don't want to see my girls get knocked up at an early age. I know it's wrong for me to think that way, but you know what? I don't care. The way things are today, with teenagers just having sex for the hell of it, is not a good thing.

I know teenagers in the neighborhood who are 17 and 18 and they tell me stuff that will make you blush. My god, sex for the hell of it, just because there's nothing else to do? How about going to a movie or something like that? But we live in a world of lust, and I think sometimes love. That's why I say the double standard issue won't be won by my daughters.

4X4's in Winter

I used to yell at drivers who drove 4x4's in the winter, "Slow down, you drive like an ass!", until I got one. Then I was driving through the snow like an ass, but you know what? A 4x4 can.

I don't know what it was, but it was fun driving down the road plowing through the snow. I knew I was pissing people off and I didn't care. It was fun. I wanted run the slow people over, yelling at them to move or I'll run their asses over. I know, I was a jackass having fun in my 4x4.

But what people don't realize is that if you go that fast in your 4x4 in the snow, when you hit those breaks on ice you're going to slide all over the road like any other vehicle. You could end up in a ditch or smashing into something, or worse killing someone just because you're having fun in the snow with your 4x4.

So you know what people? I started using my head. Slow down in the snow or you could be facing life for killing someone. It's not worth anyone's life just to have fun in the snow. And if you have your kids in the

4x4 with you when you drive like that, you need to lose your license. If you don't care enough for your kid's safety then you don't care about other people on the road. And that just makes you the asshole.

Identity Theft

We all like those commercials that show the guy moving his mouth while you hear a women's voice telling about what they bought with other people's credit. We all get a laugh. But we all know that when someone steals your identity it's not funny anymore.

Why do people steal other people's identity? Because they screwed up their own credit and now they're going to screw up someone else's. I think when people destroy other people's credit and lives, they should get life in prison. What gives you the right to screw up our lives because you've got problems?

When they get caught they're so sorry. "I didn't mean it." When they lose custody of their kids they say "I have a problem. I needed to do it. I needed drugs." How about just get a job, pay your bills and don't screw up your credit or your life? If drugs are more important to you then your kids then don't have any.

If you know you have a drug problem, don't make it worse by stealing people's identity and credit to fuel your drug problem. Go get help. You want people to feel sorry for you after you get caught because you feel bad and you're sorry for ruining that person's life? Get help instead of committing a crime. I don't feel sorry for you.

Cutting Throats for Jobs

I've worked in the construction trade for about 20 years, and I can't believe all the cut throats out there. If all of the trades stay around the same price everyone would have work. But no, people have to cut other people's prices.

I understand trades will cut their price so they can get the job, but when one company is doing a job for a $1.75 a foot and another comes in at $1.25, that's a major cut throat. It sets the price range for all the builders because they now know companies can't compete.

The only reason a company can come in with a low price like that is because they aren't paying someone. Let it be the supply store where they get their materials or they're scamming the IRS. One guy that owns a paint company told me he changes the company name every six months so he doesn't have to pay taxes. That takes balls.

And who suffers for it? The guys who do pay their taxes. I have a friend who owns his own painting company and he charges fair prices. He uses the good paint, not the watered down cheap stuff. He hardly makes any money for himself. He makes enough to pay his worker, the paint bill and the IRS. Like I said, the guy who cut throats is the one running off with all the money.

I think the IRS and other agencies need to look into some of this stuff because I do know the cut throats are the illegal aliens who can do it and not get caught. Unless the IRS really looks into it. Then the construction trades might have a chance to make it.

School Buses and Drivers

What I don't understand is why drivers have to hurry up and blow by a school bus when it's dropping our kids off. When you people see a bus and it flashes yellow lights that means slow down and get ready to stop. When you see the red lights flashing that means you have to stop about 20 feet behind the bus. Not next to it, not on its bumper, but you have to stay back 20 feet.

To the morons who blow by the bus and hit a kid, you should be shot dead right there in the street. What gives you the right to avoid stopping when a bus has its red lights flashing? You think you're above everyone else if you woke up late and you're late for work? Don't try to rush. You just might kill someone. Use your head people.

Our kids deserve to be safe when they're being picked up or dropped off by the school buses. Not to have their lives shortened because of some jackass who can't wake up in time for work has to drive like an ass to get there. So slow down and watch for the kids crossing the roads when the bus lights are flashing.

Kids, Parents and Sports

This is not always a good thing. I play in a roller hockey league and it is really fun to go out there and play. The age of our league is 16 to 40 and everyone has a good time. But then we get this loud mouth mother in the bleachers that will not shut her mouth. I can see parents cheering their kids on, but when they start yelling vulgar things to the other teams, that's just stupid.

Her son and the rest of his team were feeding off of what she was saying. Because of her mouth, and now her son's mouth, some of them got into a lot of trouble. Players on the other team started to run at them, knocking them over whenever they had the chance.

So anyway, after the game the mother kept running her mouth and the son did the same, so a guy from the other team punched him right in the mouth, causing him to bleed pretty badly. Then all hell broke out. The cops were called and players got kicked out of the league. All because of one mother who couldn't just sit there and enjoy watching her son play hockey.

So to the parents who take sports with their kids too seriously and don't let them enjoy it, stay home, or just sit there and keep your mouth shut. People don't want to hear some jackass yelling at players because they think they're cool and supporting their team. Cheering for them is one thing. Shouting obscenities and acting like an ass is another. Right?

Homes Made by Today's Standard

Today's homes aren't built like they used to be. Trust me, I know. I see what's going on after 20 years on the job. Like I said before, when construction trades start cutting throats on the prices, they also cut the quality of the work.

I think today's new home buyers know what I'm talking about. In some cities some of the building codes are different. I know in Ann Arbor, Michigan the drywall they put up doesn't need to be screwed in the middle, so your walls will bounce, smacking up against the 2x4's. The builders don't care since they made over $200,000 off of each home. Wouldn't you think the building inspectors would say something?

I'm not trying to bash the new home market, but come on, something has to be done. Someone needs to take pride when these homes are being built. I had a friend buying a new home and he wanted a standard size door that led from the back of the garage to the back yard. The builder wanted almost $500.00 to put it in. To me that's a rip off because you can get a door at your local hardware store for $80.00. When they're framing the house, all they need to do is not to put in one 2x4 and put in a 2x6 header. That's it.

And the painting! My god, some of the painters that paint these houses need to be shot. They spray everything and the walls come out so rough you can light a match off them. For the money you pay you should get the best paint job ever, but some of the paint these guys use is the worst you can get. They pay low dollars for it and you pay high prices for it. I'm telling you, these inspectors really need to crack down on some of these builders.

Or maybe they're being paid off to look the other way. Hmm, who knows?

Judging a Book by its Cover

Why is it when we look at the way people dress, some people think the worst? My 16 year old son and his friends came with me to my roller hockey game. The rink is next to a park where all the kids hang out. During our team warm ups before the game, one of my teammates took a slap shot and the puck went out of the rink.

So anyway, my son's friend found the puck next to the swing set, so like any teenager he was kicking it around, stepping on it, just having fun. When one of the ref's from the first game walked over to him and asked for it, my son's friend didn't hear the guy. Another guy came over and the next thing he knew he was knocked on his asst. By the way, my son and his friends dress up in goth clothes. Need I say more?

So the guy that runs the roller hockey league called the cops on my son and his friends. He said "Look at the way they dress. It looks like they could have a gun." Yeah right, over a plastic orange roller hockey puck. This was all happening during my hockey game. I didn't know what the hell was going on until the game was over and my wife told me.

I asked the guy who runs our league, "Did you call the cops on my kids?" He started going on about the way they dressed and that they could have robbed him for the 50 bucks he has on him. Come on people, what the hell is he talking about? Because he wears goth pants he carries a gun on him?

Just another case of judging a book by its cover. Because someone dresses weird or wears goth make-up doesn't mean they're going to rob you. They're just expressing themselves.

Our Troops

What I don't understand is why there are so many people that treat our troops so bad after they come home from a tour of duty. What gives them the right to do that? Even when a solider loses his or her life, people protest at the funeral. Don't you people have anything else better to do? Can't you show the families some respect?

To the woman who protested the war by following our President around the country, holding signs blaming the President for her son's death, come on lady, honor your son for what he did. He joined our armed forces to help keep our freedom. He made the choice to join, knowing that one day he might be going off to war. And now you blame our President.

I know people feel war is wrong, but it is real. People fighting for what they believe in. If anyone joins the armed forces they know they might be going to war. That's why they joined, to fight. Not just to get free money by standing a post somewhere in the world. That's not what the armed forces are about.

So if anyone sees a solider walking down the street, you should look at him or her and say thank you and god bless you for providing our freedom and risking your life for millions of Americans. These people are the back bone of America. It's easy for people like you to stay home and protest the war.

So to the people who protest the war, why don't you go to Iraq? Try to protest over there. Ask the troops to stop, or even better, go protest the terrorist, because they're the ones who blow everything up all over the world. Come on all you protesters, if you have the balls. Why don't you hold up signs in Pakistan or Afghanistan and yell shit at them? Then we'll see if you need our troops to save your asses.

Online Auctions

This is the best place to go and sell your junk and make some money, but also a good place to get ripped off. People put ads on the site for things they don't have, like an X-Box 360, and we get scammed. So to the auction site that sells "IT", why don't you help those people that get screwed over? You say you do, but we all know you don't. Oh yeah, people get to leave a $400.00 negative feedback.

I have seen people use false names and addresses, or they use a P.O. Box which is hard to trace. Why don't you have a better way for people to feel safer when they use your auction web site? Sure, you get your money when people sell something, but we lose out all together. And yes, we all know about your online pay site, but after they get our money it's too late. They drain their accounts and blow town. We're out money and the item we paid for.

Now instead of just making money off the people that rip people off, why don't you make sure that the buyer doesn't get ripped on your auction site? Make sure whoever sells their junk on your site has an address, not a P.O. Box. Make sure all the bank accounts are registered in that person's name as well as their address. Make us feel safer and we won't mind buying "IT" from your website.

People and Their Pets

Why is it so hard for people to take care of their pets? You're telling me that people can't take five minutes a day to walk around their yard and pick up dog shit? For the people who let the dogs shit in their house, my god, take the two minutes and open the door for them! If you say your dog isn't trained, then I suggest you train him or give him to someone who has time. You see these people on the news. My god, they're so disgusting, how can anyone live in filth like that?

I went to a lady's house one day to give her a price for painting, so she invited me in. As I entered her house I could smell this wasn't going to be good. As she was walking me through the house I had to be careful where I stepped because there were piles of dog shit everywhere. After going through just two rooms I told the lady I had to leave. She looked at me like I was kidding around so I told her that if I didn't get out of there I was going to throw up.

As we went outside so I could catch my breath, the lady asked me if I wanted to paint her house. I told her, "Lady, you need to have someone come here and tear your house down. It smells like something died in there." She got offended because I told her that, so she yelled at me to leave. As I was getting in my car she yelled "I'm telling people not to use you for house painting." So I yelled back, "Lady, if they're as bad as you, don't give them my number."

So again I ask, how can you people live that way? Remember, if you have a pet, they can't feed themselves. They can't open doors to let themselves out, and they do need a lot of attention. So please, if you have a pet or are going to get one, make sure you have the time to take care of it and not let it sit in its own shit and urine. And for god sake, make sure you feed it.

The Police and Their Tickets

I know they have a job to do, and I know that job can be tough. They go out there and put their lives on the line so we can have a safer community. I also know some cops like being jackasses when they pull people over. I've been pulled over a lot of times in my life, mostly for speeding. So I'll tell you about two times I was pulled over, once by a nice cop, and the other time by a jackass.

I was sitting at a red light, and as the light turned green I saw a police car coming towards me. He looked over at me and next thing I knew he did a u-turn. I looked in my rearview mirror and he was flashing his lights at me, so I pulled over. He got out of his car and walked over to me and asked that obvious question, "You know why I pulled you over?" I said "Because I have coffee and donuts?" Lucky he had a sense of humor. He laughed and said "You're not wearing your seatbelt."

So anyway, I did get a ticket for it and the cop told me I was one of the politest people he had pulled over that day and he thanked me for understanding why he did. That was cool to have a police officer who was that nice. All he was doing was his job, to make sure I was safe driving.

And now the jackass police officer. I pulled into a parking lot and backed into a spot. I was there waiting for my cousin because he had never been in our area and didn't know where I lived. As I was pulling out of the parking lot, a police officer came up behind me with his lights flashing and siren sounding, so I pulled over. He walked up and said "Do you know why I pulled you over?" I said no. He told me my tags were expired, and I told him that I thought I had to the end of the month. He told me that's not how it works, and then he accused me of backing into the parking spot to hide from him. I laughed and said no, I was waiting for someone. He looked at me like I was lying to him and he said "Yeah right." I told him my birthday was on the 3rd and it's now the 10th. "Why would I lie to you?" He just asked for my license, proof of insurance and registration. I couldn't find my proof of insurance so he told me he'd be right back. Ten minutes later he came up and handed me three tickets, one for the tags, one for no proof of insurance and one for a break light.

I said "Break light?" He told me it was dim and I should replace it. I just thought to myself, my god what a freaking jackass! Because of a dim light bulb he gave me a ticket. I can see about the tags, maybe the proof of insurance, but a damn light bulb? Give me a break. It's not like it was totally out. Give me a warning to fix it. He only did it because he thought I was lying to him, and that's why he's a beat cop and not a detective.

Public Restrooms

Why can't people treat a public restroom the way they treat their own bathrooms at home? I know people don't pee on their toilet seats at home, and if they do I bet they wipe it off. Can't people take pride when they use a public restroom? If you take a crap, flush the damn toilet.

What gets me the most is when people pee all over the floor. My god, you're telling me people can't make it into that big opening? I went into one restroom and I couldn't even use it. There was piss all over the seat and it was filled with crap. When you're having a bad day and you know that you're going to clog the toilet, flush the damn thing once and then again if you have to. Don't let it overflow so the next person can't even use it. No one wants to get their pants wet when they pull them down.

I feel sorry for the ones who have to clean the restrooms, but come on people, hurry up and clean them. I don't want to smell like urine after I use your facility. And to the people that really don't care, you're a freaking pig, and you're properly the most disgusting person who ever walked the face of the earth. Take pride in yourself and have the common courtesy to clean off the seat and flush when you're done. I don't want to see what you had for dinner the night before.

Cheaters

What's wrong with some of you people? Why cheat on your loved one? Is your marriage that bad? Really think about it. I understand some marriages are heading for divorce and that's fine, because I know. But when a person goes out of the way to cheat on their lover, that's just wrong.

When you're married you don't need to go out to bars with your friends. To me, the people who go out to bars just want to pick people up. I know people say they need a night out with their friends. That's fine too, but when you're out with your friends, do things that won't tempt you to cheat. I see so many married people out there shaking their asses for others. And to the guys, just because you buy a lady a drink doesn't mean you're getting laid.

Just think, if you cheat on your loved one you have a good chance of bringing home a sexual transmitted disease to your spouse, and that's not right. For what? A one night stand? If you feel the need to cheat on your spouse, you have no right being married. Why? For someone to cook and clean for you? Man, please grow up. And to the women who cheat on their men, do you think it's fair to come home pregnant with some other man's baby and then tell your man it's his baby?

That's sick, wrong and pathetic. What gives you the right to mess up your family's life? Did you ever hear of a condom? Remember the truth always comes out. For a man to think it's his kid and take care of it for years, then to have someone say it's not his can destroy a man. I don't want to sound like a jerk, but if you feel the need to cheat, you really need to have a talk with your loved one.

Explain how you feel, let each other know your feelings and what you're thinking. I hear people say that their spouse is getting fat. Well, you kind of have to say something. Don't sit by and let your marriage go down the tubes. Step up and let them know what's wrong, and that might just save your marriage. And if that doesn't work and you feel the need to cheat, get a divorce first, and then be the self centered pig that you are.

Doctors

I see some damn good doctors out there, and I also see a lot of doctors that don't give a shit about people. I like when a doctor takes his time with a person, talking to them and examining them. Then there are the ones that push you through like a herd of cattle. I went to one doctor's office and the doctor came in and said "Let's see here". He looked at my nose and throat, and in all under a minute said, "Take this and you'll get better", and then he left the room. I thought to myself "That was fast."

A week later my health got worse. I ended up going to the hospital, and I found out that I had double pneumonia. That doctor that saw me last week could have caught it earlier, instead of rushing me and treating me for a sinus problem. I hate when a doctor just gives you a pill to cover the symptoms. They need to look deeper into things before they end up killing someone.

Do the tests you need to do, doctors. I knew someone who went to a hospital for pains in his chest. The doctor really didn't do any testing and said it was indigestion. So, they walked him around the halls of the emergency room, and the next thing they knew he hit the floor and died. Come to find out the poor guy had an aneurysm, and that was what killed him.   All because they didn't do the testing.

Ok people, I'm not trying to bash our doctors. I just think they need to take more time with their patients and then they might not take out the wrong kidney, or amputate the wrong arm or leg. I have now found a great doctor and he sits with his patients, and he talks. Even if he has to work late, he does. If all doctors did that there wouldn't be as many screw-ups and people would have a better chance to live.

Different Lifestyles

A lot of people that see a gay person freak out. Why? Because they're different. Who cares? They are living life the way they want, and who are we to judge them? Most of them have great jobs, they pay taxes and they should have their rights just like anyone else. I hear people say that the Bible says it's wrong, and that God made Adam & Eve, not Adam & Steve. And here we go people judging people.

If they're not flaunting it around you, just leave it alone. They like their lifestyle and who are we to say different? If God doesn't like it, he will deal with them on judgment day, just like he will deal with you for bashing them and judging them. I'm not saying its right, all I'm saying is that people have a right to choose the way they want to live. And that's fine with me.

As long as no one is getting hurt, who cares? If they want to get married let them. If they want to adopt kids, I say let them do it. I believe they will raise a child better then some of the other people in this world. Just because someone has a different life style doesn't mean they're bad people. They're just different and no one has the right to bash them for it.

This is a free country and everyone has rights. I don't care who it is. The only people that don't deserve any rights are child molesters and murderers, who all deserve death. So come on people, there is so much more to life then judging people with a different life style.

Car Insurance and Your Credit Score

What the hell is this about? Why should our credit score effect our car insurance policy? They say it helps you save money, I say bull shit. If we don't smash our cars for a year, then we should save money. I'm paying for an insurance policy, not taking out a loan. Whoever came up with this idea needs to be slapped in the head, and hard.

Let me get this right, if I have a low credit score, I have to pay a higher rate and if someone has a high credit score they pay a lower rate? Ok, what if some jerk has a bad driving record and a good credit score? Does that mean he still pays less then me, even if my driving record is good and my credit score is bad? This is wrong. Our credit score should have nothing to do with our driving.

Ok, tell us the truth. Is this a good way for all these car insurance companies to make more money? That's what it seems like, doesn't it? I guess their covering their asses by making us pay high rates, because they keep getting scammed every year. Why don't you guys raise the rates of the people who scam you, or the ones who you think are scamming you? Don't take it out on the good people that don't scam you.

I'm sure you big shots have a great education. If you're all sitting around thinking shit up, thinking of ways to make more money, that's fine. But remember, there are a lot of people driving without insurance because the rates are too high. I'll tell you what, why don't you think of a way to help people afford car insurance, instead of just making money?

Our Detroit Mayor

I know people think he wasn't the right choice for the mayor of Detroit, but I beg to differ. It will take time since he is sort of young, but I know he'll pull through for the city. Give him a few years. I know there was a lot said about him ripping off the city, but you know, it could be worse. At least he paid some of the money back.

I think it was cool that he got the Super Bowl here, and he will turn the city around in years to come. What gets me now is that everyone is giving him shit for wanting to fix up the mayor's mansion. Come on people, do you think they should let the White House go to waste because it will cost money to fix? Same thing here. The mayor of Detroit has to represent the city and he has a lot of people coming and going from the mansion.

If the city counsel will work with the mayor and vise versa, they will move along a lot faster. Try not to cut the jobs of police officers and firemen, we need them out there. Let the big shots of the city take a pay cut.

Let me give you a little advice for when scrap yards are buying stolen copper and other scrap metals. You, the city of Detroit, should have the courts help to seize those businesses and then let you, the city of Detroit, take it over. If any more people get caught stealing copper and other scrap from the city or businesses, the city should have the right to seize those peoples' homes and other assets. Sell it to help make repairs to the city and the businesses that were stolen from. I bet that will help stop people from stealing from the city and businesses in our great city of Detroit.

Santa Claus

What gets me is the people who have a problem with a fat man in a red suit that only comes out once a year during Christmas time. There are people out there that say Santa Clause is not god, and we're wrong for worshiping an object. Ok people, get over it.

We all know Santa Claus is not a god, and we don't worship him. It's a Christmas decoration that people use that represents Christmas. Yes, we all know its Jesus' birthday and we respect that, but we all use Santa for the kids to have fun. It's fun for us to let them think he comes down the chimney to leave gifts for them. That's it, nothing else.

You know what else bugs me about these people? When they hear that Christmas song "He knows when you are sleeping and he knows if you're awake". They start freaking out because Santa is not a god. We know he's not. He is a fictional character, that's it. Santa is not real and he doesn't really climb down your chimney. You people are the freaks, let it go.

It seems like you people think he's real by the way you talk and act. You must have better things to do then sit there and complain about Santa. He's a fictional character. My god, worry about your own lives and if you don't want your kids having fun, that's your problem. Don't worry about what other people do around the holidays and how they celebrate. Remember, you have your god given right, and so do we.

So please let us enjoy our holidays and we won't complain that you people are a bunch of ball busting stick in the mud freaks. And oh yeah, god bless us all.

Our Elections

Ok, to all of you elected officials, I hate hearing the way you go about getting elected. If you do something then that the gay community will vote for you, or the black community will, or even the women of a community. How about what you can do for all the people in our country instead of just for a race or for the women?

We are all in this together, right? So why can't we have someone that is there for all the people of this country? I bet you will have a better chance of winning. I know people are still fighting for their rights in this country and when its election time, you speak out to the people you want to help and try to get their votes, which is fine.

But aren't we all supposed to be equal? That's what I thought. I find it hard to believe that we can't all come together and get what this country needs. Let's not look at life styles, race or even the men and women issues. Let's look at it like we are all humans and we all need the same things in life. And then, just then, we might have a better country to live in, where we all are equals. Because after all, we are all human.

Another thing, instead of all the mud slinging and attacks on each other, why don't you just tell us your plan and how you'll change the economy and make our children's education better? Its funny watching you politicians make fools out of yourselves, blaming each other for stupid shit that happened over ten years ago. How about you just stick to the matters at hand and what we need done today to help fix our own state or country?

Charity Scams

Why do people have to scam good people? I know there are a lot of crooks out there and all they care about are themselves, but you jerks are ripping off the people that have no money themselves, and most of all the senior citizens. You take money from those who only have social security checks and barely have enough to survive.

I think when you people get caught for scamming you should lose all of your assets. The courts should sell your homes, cars, land and anything else of value that you own, and give the money back to the people you scammed. Whatever is left over, if any, should go to a charity that you said you were from. I hate seeing you assholes get off light for what you've done. You go to court after you're caught and start crying to the judge, and then you get probation and have to pay restitution that doesn't even add up to the damages you've caused.

If you scam artists really use your heads you can open your own businesses and make good on it. You guys plan out your scam. Why don't you really think about how to make it work legally so you don't rip off good people? You just might make the money you want. And to the people who get scammed, please look into everything before you give away your money. If you don't know, ask a relative or a lawyer to check it out. If it's too good to be true, it can cost you thousands.

Banks and Their Fees

I hate it when the banks make money off us. Why do we have to pay over $4.00 in ATM fees to use a bank that is not ours? It costs me $2.00 for the bank that owns the ATM, and then my bank charges me another $2.00 for the transaction. That's a rip off. First they tell me they have locations everywhere, so I figured "Good." Then I find the closest one is two miles away.

Ok I know it's not that far, but don't we all look for convenience? And what about the NSF fees? I wrote a check out and when it was cashed, I went in the hole for 24¢. I put the money in the next day and they still charged me $35.00 for going under. I would understand if it were over $50.00 in the hole. Charge me the $35.00, but for a lousy 24¢? Give me a damn break.

I think they need to sit back and think about how they run their banks. They need to give people a chance to make it. The way things are going in this economy, people can't get ahead. The banks know when we put money in our accounts when we have direct deposit, so they know the money would be in there in the next day or so.

I like how some of these banks say free checking. Yeah right. Only if you have a minimum of $50.00 to $300.00 kept in it all times. I think we need a bank that would really help the people by letting certain fees go. They could have a lot more customers by taking away or lowering the ATM fees, and to waive the NSF for people with direct deposit, or if it's under that $35.00 fee. Think how cool it could be if there was a bank that really cared about the people, and less about how they can make money off of us.

High School Shootings

What the hell is wrong with these kids that have to run into a school and start shooting other kids? My god, if you're thinking of doing something that dumb you really need to talk to someone, get yourself some help. Taking innocent kids hostage or shooting them because you were being teased? Come on, that's really stupid.

I tell you what... If you feel you have to storm a school, think about it for a minute. There are a lot of people in there that can't defend themselves. So after you think about it, and you really think you have to do it, go storm a police station. If you think that you're big and bad and not afraid of dying then storm the police station. Then we will see how far you'll make it. I would rather see them try it against people who are armed and can shoot back.

I'm not trying to start trouble, but I'm sick of seeing all these kids thinking of killing other kids in a school. Killing innocent kids that can't defend themselves is wrong. I'm just saying that if they have the guts to kill kids, then they should try it against people who can shoot back. For the kids who get caught making threats, they need to be prosecuted to the full extent of the law. Let them sit in there so they can think about what the hell they were going to do.

The people who do try to kill innocent kids need to be put to death. If you didn't already shoot yourself first (and to me that's a coward) don't shoot yourself. If you've got the guts to do that, then you should have the guts to take your medicine and face the music.

Schools need to think about our children's safety. After that first bell rings they need to lock all the doors, and no one will be allowed in. If someone comes to the school they need to be buzzed in by the front office. If they see a freak in the parking lot walking around and they know he doesn't belong there, call the damn cops. Report the freak so no one else gets killed.

Video Games

Wake up America, and minimize the time your children play video games. I know they're fun and I know adults think their kids are staying out of trouble if they stay home and play them. But think of the stuff that they're missing out on. A lot of kids don't have any friends, or if they, do they sit around and play those damn games with them.

It's not healthy for our kids to sit for hours and play video games. No, I'm not talking about they will become fat and lazy. I'm talking about their mental health and the way they sit there and let life pass them by. There's so much more to do in life then sitting there all day or after school. They need to run around, make friends, play sports and do something else with their time.

Give them the right push. Make them see there is more outside activities then inside. When they get older some of these kids don't know anything, and they have a harder time understanding life and people. After all, they've led a sheltered life with no friends and haven't learned responsibility.

They'll depend on other people to do things for them. Ok yes, they will become lazy.

I just think kids of today need to get out more. You never see kids playing in the streets like we did when we where younger. I asked my kids if they ever played kick the can or man on the moon, and they just looked at me like I was an idiot. Then I thought to myself, damn they're living a sheltered life. I had a talk with them and now they have a limited time for video games and internet.

Now they have so many friends, they do a lot more outdoor activities then indoors, and I'm proud of them. It took time but it worked. They're having fun, and now I just have to keep reminding them to be in by nine on a school night. To me that's a good trade off.

Abortion

This is a very touchy subject and a lot of people have trouble with it. I know there are a lot of religious people out there that fight against it. To me the women have the right to do what they want. If someone got raped and pregnant they should have the right to get an abortion. I know people say give it up for adoption. To me that's wrong to make someone carry a baby from a rapist. They need time to get over what happened and not have a nine month reminder of that day.

I feel sorry for the women who have abortions because they have to live with it everyday. They don't need a bunch of jackasses reminding them of how bad they already feel. To me if they're not ready or can't afford it, or even if they're teenagers, they should have the right to make the decision of what they want to do. And it should be done in the beginning of the pregnancy, not near the end.

To all you stupid people that have to stand outside a clinic and protest, you're no better then anyone else to say stuff to the people as they're walking in, or to throw stuff at the workers. What about the jackasses that killed a doctor or fire bombed their building? How would you like it if I decided to protest your church or organization? What if you pissed me off and I fire bomb your building and churches? Does that make me right? No, and it doesn't make you right either.

So do us all a favor, stay home, read your Bible and let God decide what to do. Because you're not doing anything but making yourselves look like a bunch of morons. Let these poor women make their decisions, and let's not make them feel any worse then they already do.

I also hate hearing about how the government should step in on this issue. To me the government needs to stay out of the doctors offices. Let the people have the right to make their own choices, without anyone giving them anymore shit for doing what they need to do.

Credit Card Offers

Is it me or does this happen to everyone? I applied for a credit card and they turned me down, and I thought "Oh well." But now I'm getting credit card offers from the same place that turned me down. It's like they're teasing me with them, and it's starting to get on my nerves.

I don't understand. If they turned me down, why are they sending more offers? They know they're not going to give it to me. Why bother? I think they just like hassling me. So anyway, I wrote on it and told them to stick it where the sun doesn't shine. After that I didn't receive any more offers from them. I think some of these companies are just stupid and they need to either give us one or just leave us alone.

But the bottom line is that I'm glad they turned me down. I don't need another bill that will take twenty years to pay off. I learned that if you can't pay cash for it, you don't need it.

Cola Wars

Coke wins, all others suck. Thank you for your time. Have a coke and a smile and shut-up.

Halloween

This is the night kids dress up in costumes and run the streets for candy, a night of fun and excitement. To other adults, because of their beliefs they think it's an evil night and the kids shouldn't take part in it. I don't understand why some of these people have to ruin the night for the kids. It's not an evil night, but a way for kids to have fun. They only get to do it once a year.

If it were really an evil night, don't you think they would run around and cut people's heads off, instead of getting candy? I understand people worry about what's in the candy and if someone did something to it. Instead of the parents checking the candy or taking it to a local place that does it for them, they won't even let their kids go or they throw out the candy when the kids get home. To me I think a lot of parents are lazy and just don't want anything to do with it.

To the ones who won't let their kids go around the neighborhood because they think its evil, why do you have a hallelujah night at church? The kids still dress up and run around the church getting candy from people. Sounds like the same thing to me. The only difference is you cover up the real meaning of Halloween by changing the name of it for your benefit, and instead of running the streets, they run the church.

People should let their kids decide if they want to go around the neighborhood with their friends instead of being forced to do what the parents want, like making them going to church or just sit home.

Internet Predators

How stupid can people be? You know the police are monitoring the Internet chat rooms to help protect our children from those sick perverted freaks who get their kicks trying to meet or have sex with under aged girls. I think if those stupid people get caught, they should be prosecuted to the full extent of the law.

Let them sit in prison for twenty years so they can really think about what they were going to do. Or they need to be shot in the head. To me they're no better then those sick freaks that rape little kids. You know what they would have done if they did get a chance to meet an under aged girl who didn't let her parents know where she was going or who she would be with.

To all the parents, no matter who you are, you really need to monitor your kids on the internet. I always do surprise inspections on my kids, and if they don't let me see their My Space or email accounts, I won't let them go on the computer, make phone calls or even leave the house to visit their friends.

So yeah, you could say I would ground them. I don't give them the chance to call or go over a friend's house so they can change or delete their My Space or email.

I have always told them to be honest with my wife and me, and never give us a reason to believe they're lying to us. They will face serious consequences by losing all of their time on the internet or phone calls to their friends. I don't sit there and read all their emails. I just see who they're from. If I don't know who they're talking about, I ask questions. I also make sure they don't give out too much information on their My Space account, like what school they go to or our address and city.

I think the kids and I have a good understanding about what's going on, and they're all pretty honest with me and the wife, and that's the main thing. We have great communication together and there is a lot of trust. They know I won't ground them for the petty and stupid stuff. I'm not one of those over protective parents. I just make sure they're safe and taking care of themselves. Like I've said before, keep an open mind with your kids and trust them. I'm telling you, it's best for the whole family.

People Who Think They're Doing the Planet a Favor

I always hear about people who want to save the planet. To me that's cool. People who care, they ride bikes because they believe a car is killing the environment. I respect those people and what they believe in. But the ones that piss me off are the kind of people that tell me that they won't get a car because it's killing our planet, but yet, they come to me and ask for a ride or they ask other people. To me that's just a freeloader that doesn't want to get a job and pay for their own car or the insurance. They would rather tell us that we're killing the planet. That's right, we're killing it. To me they're still coming along for the ride and helping me.

I think the planet is really going to be fine. Our planet has been around for a very long time and when it feels like something needs to be cleaned, that's when mother nature steps in. Then we have our hurricanes, thunderstorms and even the occasional tsunami so she can clean herself up. Our planet really knows how to take care of itself. I just think some people go a little overboard. But yet, they really do care, and I just want to say thanks people.

To the people that go out of their way to protest the oil drillers in the oceans, you think you're doing the planet good, but really think about how much diesel fuel your boat pumps out. Some of the things you people do doesn't make any sense to me.

Emergency Vehicles

How stupid are some of you people out there? When you see or hear an emergency vehicle coming you know you have to stop and pull over to the side of the road. I know it's hard if you're at an intersection at a red light, but the people that don't try to move out of the way or don't give the right of way are morons.

The other day I saw an ambulance trying to get to the hospital by my house and when he was trying to pass through the intersection, the left turn lane light turned green. Everyone was trying to make their turn and wouldn't give the ambulance a chance to make his turn. So to the idiots that think they have the right to do that, they should try to get your plate number and report you to the police, so they can suspend your driver's license for a year.

To me that seems fair. If you think you have the right to play god and ruin a person's chance at life because of you not giving the right of way to an emergency vehicle, you should pay the price of being a jackass. What if it were one of your family members in that ambulance and people didn't give them a chance to live? Wouldn't that piss you off? So people, please use common sense the next time you see an emergency vehicle coming down the road.

Car Accidents

I know the police have a job to investigate car crashes, and know that if someone was killed in a car crash they have to take even longer to investigate and they keep the roads closed. But when it's just a fender bender on the express way, they need to get those vehicles out of the way so they don't have a fifty mile back up.

Especially during rush hour. I know you guys have your hands full when there is a fender bender, but get the damn cars out of the way. If you did that everything will go smoother for everyone. To the people that had the car crash, you need to learn not to swerve in and out of lanes. Some of you drive like you think you'll get home faster if you do ninety miles per hour down the freeways. Guess what, you won't. I know a lot of people want to get home after a hard days work and I understand that, but to risk your life and the other people's lives on the roads, that's just stupid.

Again, it pisses me off that people think they have the right to do what they want on the roads. Who gives you the right to play god and decide to take a chance with other people's lives? Even when I have my kids in the car and people can see them, they still ride my ass to try to make me go faster. Here is a clue jackass… I can only go as fast as the car in front of me. You people don't have the right to risk my kids lives, so the next time you feel you need to do a hundred, don't. Now I do understand why there is road rage and you people get your ass kicked because of it.

To the people that have to stare at the accident while driving by, learn to keep your eyes on the road. Half of you morons cause more accidents because you have to look at the side of the road where the crash is, instead of what's going on in front of you.

Attention Deficit Disorder

I feel it's my duty to let everyone know that these doctors really need to look harder at our kids who they might think they have A.D.D. I see a lot of these kids today get put on medications for it, and I believe the doctors need to really examine our kids a little better. I think a lot of kids are just plain lazy and don't care for certain things in life.

Really think about it. I know someone whose kid is labeled A.D.D. To me the kid is just lazy. When he needs to get up for school he can't. When he needs to do his homework he can't. Does that mean the kid is A.D.D.? No he's not. I heard the kid can wake up at 5a.m. to go to a festival with his friends and can get up to play Dungeons & Dragons with his friends. When the kid wants to do something for himself that's fun, he's fine. But when it's time for school work and house chores he has A.D.D. Quick, give the kid a pill! Bullshit!!!

The kid just doesn't care about school or if you're talking about something that he doesn't like. And how do I know that? Because he told me. But if we talk about video games and Dungeons and Dragons, he will talk your ear off. To me that's just a kid being lazy and wanting to do things his own way, and I understand that. So let's teach our kids what they need to do in life, instead of giving them a stupid pill, which could end up killing them.

I'm not saying all kids are just being lazy. I know some kids really do have it, but I think they need to look a little deeper into the matter. That might just save a few lives.

Domestic Violence

Why do people have to beat their loved ones? To show how tough they are, to feel like a bigger person, or is it a power trip? I think when people are abusive they need to be in prison for life. I see and hear about women and kids getting beat for no reason, and even men being abused by women. I see people get restraining orders against those people and we all know that doesn't work. People have to go live in shelters so they can't be found.

When there is a domestic violence case and someone is beat half to death, the person that did it should be arrested on the spot and never released. I mean, don't even give them a bond to get out. A lot of the time that person gets out and tries to hunt down the other person and kills them. Our courts need to really start cracking down on people for their actions, especially when there are kids involved. Nothing breaks my heart more then when an innocent child gets beat an inch from death.

All because the dad or mom has a drinking problem or they have mental issues? To me it's sick that they take their frustrations out on a little kid. People that abuse kids need to be shot. A person that is with a violent lover really needs to look at what may happen if they have a child with that person. If they're abusive to you, you know they will be abusive to your kid.

To the sick freaks that beat an infant to death because it cries too much, you sick ass freaks need to be treated the same way. I think you should be beat to death. And if that person has caused multiple deaths, they need to be beat within an inch of their life and brought back to good health, and then beaten again until they die. Let them know how it feels when they can't defend themselves just like a baby can't.

If you feel so frustrated that you can't handle it any more, put the baby down in their crib and walk away. Go have a smoke, cool off, and then attend to the baby when you calm down.

Gold Diggers

People make me laugh when I hear that they've been taken for a ride, when they knew the girl was using them for their money. When you have a gorgeous woman that wants to be with you and you have a lot of money, you better watch yourself. I have seen a few people go broke because of gold diggers.

When you start spending a lot of money and the woman doesn't tell you to slow down or she keeps making you buy her everything she sees, that tells me you might be dating a gold digger. I've seen a few buddies lose their asses. If you don't slow down and see what's happening, your going to be broke before you know it. One girl went out with one of my buddies and she took him for a ride. He lost every penny he had saved. As soon as the money ran out she was gone. We use to make fun of him and told him he had the most expensive hooker in the world. Honestly, it would have been cheaper to get a $600.00 a night call girl, twice a month.

Its funny how someone can help you destroy your life financially, then not give a shit about you after it's all gone. You think someone loves you and cares for you and they just walk away finding another sucker to sponge off of. This kind of person doesn't have any morals or a decent bone in their body. I'm not just talking about how women do it. There are a lot of men that do it to women. Many of you need to look at the type of person your with. If they make you spend a lot of money on them and they're not reaching for their wallets, they might just be taking you for a ride. And there is nothing illegal about.

Here is a big clue, if your bills aren't being paid and if the bank is sending you a letters of foreclosure, that would be a good time to look at if you're dumping all your money on someone. And if you are, you better hope a good piece of ass is worth losing everything for.

The Automotive Big 3

Everyone remembers when they heard the words The Big 3. They knew it was GM, Ford and Chrysler. Its funny how times have changed and everyone thinks that they are still The Big 3. But if you really look at it, the top 3 now are Toyota, Daimler Chrysler and Honda. Honda beat GM by a few cents, but to me it counts. GM isn't in the top three any more and Ford isn't even in the top six. My god, even Nissan and Fiat are better then Ford as of September 30th of 2006.

I understand you have to make job cuts and close plants around the country, but really think of all the workers you have cut. Why don't you guys think of ways to save peoples jobs, rather then cutting them loose? I think if you higher up big shots take pay cuts and less vacations, you could save a few hundred jobs. Why don't you guys make cars people can afford? Does it really cost a lot of money to make a car? I didn't think so. Why not cut your prices a little lower then what you sell it for?

Just as an example, if a car cost you three thousand dollars to make, why don't you sell it for six thousand dollars instead of fifteen thousand? You may think it would be a loss, but think how many of them people would buy. That would be a big sales boost for you. And please, when you do make your cars, why the hell do we get a stupid donut tire? For the price you sell your cars for we should get that fifth rim and tire.

Well anyway, I know it's a dream, because that would never happen. So I will now wake up and smell the coffee, and some of you American automakers better do the same, because the foreign automaker is kicking your ass.

Depressed People

I know there are a lot of people who are really depressed, and they should be on medication for it because of a chemical imbalance. But the people who *think* they're depressed need to look at their lives a little closer. I see people get depressed for the most stupid shit, like their jobs or their family lives or they think nothing is going their way.

I understand life is hard, but if you're going through life thinking that a pill will make your life be better, you're mistaken. Why take a pill to help cover things up? Why don't you fix the problems that are causing you to feel that way? If your job has you depressed and you can't handle it anymore, I think its time for a career change. Get a job that would suit you better and that won't cause you a lot of headaches. So basically, you should have a job with less stress.

I know there can be a lot of problems in the home, so again, instead of taking a pill to make you feel better or to cover up your home life problems, you should take the problem head on. If you're having a problem with your spouse you should sit down and have a long talk with them. Get it all out and let them know how you feel. If your spouse loves you like they say they do, they will listen to you. I guarantee you will feel much better. If your spouse treats you like shit and they don't care about you, you should really look at if you should be in a relationship that is unfair to you.

All I'm trying to say is that people need to look long and hard at their lives. Instead of popping pills all day to make life better, do something about it. Don't be afraid to step up and speak your mind. After all, you need to express feelings and to take charge of your life.

Social Security Benefits

Who the hell decides who get benefits? It's funny, you get a statement every year from Social Security and it tells you what you're entitled to for disability or retirement, right? Well, if you're disabled and can't work any more you're entitled to shit. I have seen so much bullshit that it would make you sick.

This guy I knew had a heart attack and almost died, so his doctors told him to retire or collect S.S. benefits. He applied and got turned down. They told him he could still work so the guy said oh well, and went back to work. The next thing he knew, he had another heart attack and was hospitalized. And the bastards at Social Security still turned him down. To me that's bullshit.

So anyways, who decides who gets S.S. benefits? People pay into a fund for their benefits and I think if someone is really sick they should be able to collect on them. Even if it's for a year or two, they're entitled to it. After they get better they can go back to work and stop collecting their S.S. checks. There are a lot of people out there that get sick and can't work. When the paychecks stop coming in, the bills keep piling up and some lose their homes. All because some jackass determines who gets benefits and who doesn't.

Death Penalty

Ok, now I'm going to hit a few nerves of some people. I think they need to bring back the death penalty for a lot of reasons. Like pedophiles, rapists, murderers and drunk drivers who kill people, even on their first offense. It should be a federal law instead of a state law. People want crime to come down in their cities, this is a way to do it.

Do you think these criminals care about jail? They think a few years aren't anything and they're out. If the government starts putting these criminals to death, the crime rate will start dropping. Then these bastards will think twice about molesting our children and breaking other laws that hurt or kill innocent people.

I know people say that the death penalty is the wrong way to bring down the crime rate, but if you think about it, it's the best way to make our children safer. After all, that's what we really want. Law makers need to sit back and really do their jobs and think about the safety of the people.

Still, give the criminal his day in court and if he is found 100% guilty, then death it is. I would also like to add that the victim's family should be the ones that push the button to put the criminal to death. And if they can't do it, please call me and I would be more then happy to push the button. I'm sorry to say that I would be happy, but after all, it shows how much I care for the children that are the victims.

Our State Lottery

Did you ever get a lottery ticket and at the top of the ticket it said 100% of the lottery profits go to the public schools? To me that doesn't seem true if the lottery made over $667 million in the last year alone like they said it did. And don't forget about the school taxes people pay for. Why in the hell are there teacher strikes and teachers without contracts? I understand that the lotto profits pay for computers and stuff, so why don't they take care of our teacher's first, instead of spending all the money on junk that they don't need?

Don't take that out of context, because first and foremost we need teachers, and then textbooks, more then computers and basketballs. Each city that sells lottery tickets should get the profits and the state should let them spend it on their own school districts where they need it most. Of course, the state government should watch over the cities and how they spend it to make sure they get the right stuff and what they need, like teachers and books. To me that would solve a lot of the stupid stuff like the teacher strikes.

Teachers Having Sex with Students

Here is a good topic, I hear people talking about that 14 year boy who had sex with that hot teacher. A lot of teenagers I know were saying that boy was stupid for ruining a good thing. They were saying how lucky he was to have a nice piece of ass. The thing that gets me the most was that the woman teacher got a few months in jail. That's it, months, not years.

If it was a male teacher that had sex with a girl, that guy would be in prison for life. To me something does seem right. Because she was a woman, she got a lighter sentence. My god, that boy was 14, not 16! She is a child molester, not just a sex offender.

I know there are a lot of boys who dream of having sex with a hot older woman, but come on, it's still wrong. She is still a pedophile and needs to be punished to the full extent of the law. Like I said before, if it was a male teacher he would have hung by his balls and been beaten for it.

But since it was a female teacher, she gets off easy, and I guess the boy gets a high five from all his friends and some male adults who think he was a lucky kid. In my own opinion this topic doesn't fall under the double standard issue.

Teenagers of Today

It's funny, when I talk to some of the teenagers in the neighborhood they make a lot of sense to me. It's amazing what some of these teenagers think about today. Some think people are jackasses for judging them because of how they dress or how they look. One teenager told me that if he walked in front of one guy's house again, he was told the guy will shoot him because of how the teenager looked and dressed. That guy has problems if he needs to threaten a teenager.

Some were wondering what will happen to them if they die and where they will they go. I have seen some teenagers sit in the rain just thinking about life, while some sit on a couch and screw up their lives by taking drugs. Some people say the kids will follow in their parents' footsteps, but I don't think that's true. I think they will follow what's in their hearts and minds, if they use them. Some teenagers think they won't amount to much in life, and that's when it all starts. They live their lives like shit because they think people don't care about them. I think if we try to steer them down the right paths in life and talk to them to let them know there are options in life, they'll have a much better chance of making the right decisions.

I asked some of the teenagers why they are worried about dying. Why worry about where you're going after you die? I told them they should think about living, not dying. There is so much more to life to think about. They should think about what they want in life and where they would like to be in ten to twenty years. I also told them whatever they set their minds to they can accomplish. Some teenagers are confused about religion. I just told them they would have to be true to their hearts and to themselves and have a little faith, and that will help sort out most of life for them.

Remember, in life you have to make yourself happy and do that any way you can. That's the best part of life, and when you do that, the people around you will feel it as well. But the bottom line is that if you don't have a handle on the reality of life, you could be lost. To the teenagers that keep your feelings bottled up, please learn how to deal with your feelings. If not you could make yourself so stressed out that it could make you physically and mentally ill. Always try to talk to someone you can trust, and never feel ashamed or embarrassed of anything. Don't worry about what other people think. Be true to your heart. Never pressure yourself into anything. Just sit back and take life as it comes, and leave all the drama in life behind you.

Some teenagers think that school is unfair. I hear the excuse that teachers don't like them and that's why they're getting bad grades. So, I asked them if they do their homework and turn it in on time. Some said yes and some said they didn't, or it wasn't finished all the way. Well, to me it doesn't sound like the teachers hate you. If you're not caring enough to do the work, they have about 30 other kids they have to help. The kids that do turn in their homework and show they're trying will get more attention. If you're having a problem in that class and don't understand it, don't be afraid to ask for help.

Well, what else can I say about the teenagers of today? I think teenagers need to stop looking too deep into everything that happens in life. Today you hear about them cutting, burning, or even worse, killing themselves. All because of life not being the way they want it. I do understand that teenagers go through a lot. But come on, to self inflect wounds?

One girl told me her life is bad because her parents hate her and don't let her do anything, and because she gets grounded for not cleaning her room or for coming in too late. Well guess what, clean your room. Be in on time when you're told to. It's not that they hate you. They are teaching you to be responsible for what you do. If they hated you they would let you run wild and not care what you do. Everything in life is a teaching process for you to do well and to not mess up your life.

Some teenagers will cause self infected wounds to help relieve the pressures of life. Come on, grow up and use your heads. Causing wounds mean you're unstable and need help. When you feel like hurting yourself, you really need to talk to someone like a counselor, a teacher or a parent. Don't always run to a friend, because they don't know everything. They will tell you what they think you should hear, and it can make things harder for you because they don't have any true experience themselves. Always remember, people do care about you and how you feel. And your parents do need to listen to you when you're having a problem.

When teenagers talk to someone they need to remember to be truly honest and really open up to their parents, counselor or teacher. Teenagers need to know they can trust you. That way they can have the best help for themselves. I always tell my teenagers that they can talk to me about anything from drugs, sex and most of all, about the things that happen in their lives. They do know that cutting or hurting themselves is not going to help anything in life. They need to be able to think for themselves and we have to be there to guide them down the right paths. Not force them, but to make them understand that there is no such thing as shit life, or a bad life, or life that is not fair. There is only life and what you make of it. Whatever you choose and do as a teenager will affect you when you hit your adulthood.

Disciplining Your Kids

Why are there so many idiots that think spanking your kids is wrong? Back when I was a kid we got the belt if we were bad. Did that make my father a bad man? I don't think so. When my father disciplined me and my brothers he would always use the belt, never his hand. My father taught us the hand is for showing love and reaching out to your kids, and that's why he used the belt.

Nowadays you get these idiots who think if you spank your kids it is child abuse. That's not true. Look at when we were growing up. We were spanked for what we did wrong and we learned from it, and we hardly ever did it again.

Today you see these parents put their kids in a time out or they count to 3. To me that's just stupid. Now you see why there are so many messed up kids today. They don't really learn when you give them a time out or if you count to three. When I hear parents count to their kids I start to laugh, because half of the time the kid will finish the count, making the parent look like an ass. That's why I think the parents who count to three are idiots. Now if you give a kid a little smack on the ass, they will listen to you and know they did something wrong. When you put a kid in a time out or if you count to three, the kid thinks you're a joke. I don't mean beat your kid, but to show them that you as a parent mean business. Don't use brutal force, just show them they messed up and not to do it again.

I also know there are a lot of kids that say they will call the police if you touch them. Well you know what? Who cares? As the parent you need to tell that kid that they can call whomever they want, because in the long run you can ask that smart ass kid where they are going to live, or tell them you hope they like juvenile hall. Remember, you run your kid's life, not your kids running your life.

Now to the people who want to arrest the parents of those kids who break the law. Are you kidding me? You need to get your head out of your asses. First you want to arrest the parents for spanking their kids, and now you want to arrest them for their kids breaking the law. My god, we can't do anything if they are bad, and now you arrest us if they screw up. I hope your kid breaks the law so it can come back on to you people. I think some of you law makers need to go back to school.

Epilogue

Ok, now you've read it. If you made it to this point, you were very interested in what I had to say, or you are so pissed off that you wanted to finish this book because I hit a few nerves. Please don't think I wrote this book to piss people off or to upset families or organizations. I wrote this so people can really see how they act towards each other, and to show there are more things we can do to protect our children.

But to tell you the truth, I did get a big kick out of writing this book. It felt great to speak my mind. I like speaking out to people so they can really see the things that make this country what it is today. We have whiners, cry babies and people who can't mind their own damn business. We have racist idiots, religious fanatics, and all kinds of stupid people. Now if everyone could actually see how they act and if they could change just a little bit, not a whole lot, just a little, this world could be a better place to live.

Or you know what, who cares what the world thinks? Let's just take care of our own country. Our true country name should be the United States of Embarrassments until we solve our own problems. When people change, then once again we can be proud of our country and the people in it. I just want people to see how foolish they can be. I think as people we should have respect for each other and not worry about race, religion, and all the other bullshit that goes on in life.

We are all equal in the eyes of God, right? Then we should all be equals in the eyes of each other. When everyone realizes that, we all will be better as humans and not thought of as jackasses in a country that can't take care of its own people. So be kinder to each other, stop judging one another, and teach your kids well, with honesty and respect, because what you teach them today they will take with them in the future.

I would love to hear from you. Please let me know what you think of Brutal Honesty. I will answer all emails and any questions at honestybrutal@yahoo.com, or even if you would just like to leave a comment.

www.ingramcontent.com/pod-product-compliance
Lightning Source LLC
Chambersburg PA
CBHW030530020726
47494CB00004B/1300